Because
everyone loves
a good story...

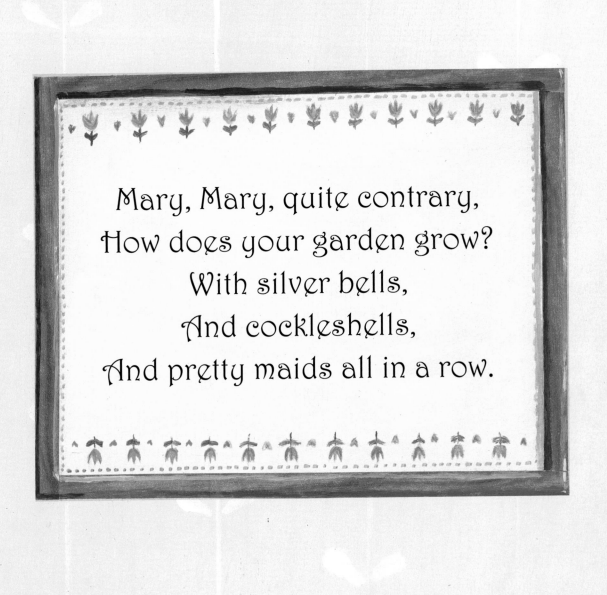

Mary, Mary, quite contrary,
How does your garden grow?
With silver bells,
And cockleshells,
And pretty maids all in a row.

For Suzanne: every garden should have such a splendid bloom—A.McQ.
To Ethan and Frankie with love—R.B.

For Lulu's cupcake recipe;
instructions on how to
make a Mary Mary doll
and much more...
go to www.alannabooks.com

First published in paperback in the UK in 2016 by
Alanna Books
46 Chalvey Road East,
Slough, Berkshire, SL1 2LR

www.alannabooks.com

ISBN: 978-1-907825-125
Printed and bound in China

Lulu Loves Flowers

Anna McQuinn
Illustrated by Rosalind Beardshaw

ALANNA BOOKS

Lulu loves her book of garden poems.
Her favourite is the one about Mary Mary.

Lulu wants a flower garden too.
Mummy says there's space near
her vegetables.

Lulu gets books about gardens
from the library.

She chooses her favourite flowers
from the books.

Mummy writes them in a list.

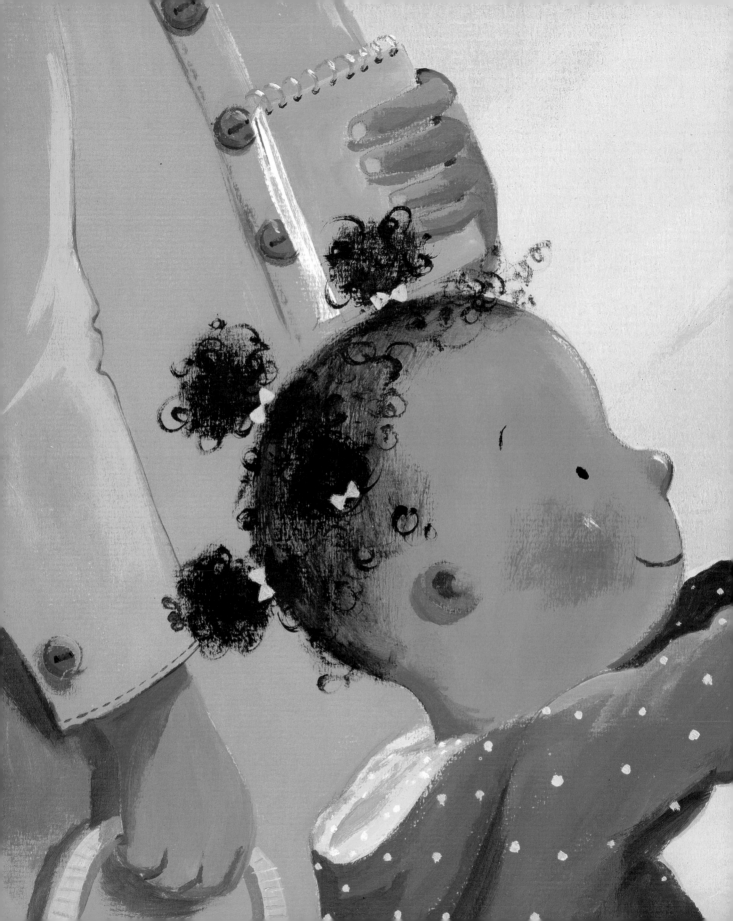

They go to the garden centre to buy seeds.

Lulu and Mummy plant the seeds.

The packets mark where each flower
is planted.

Lulu checks next day, but she can't
see any flowers yet.

She will have to wait
a long time for them to grow.

While she waits, Lulu makes her own flower book.

Mummy types the Mary Mary poem
and Lulu glues it in.

Lulu makes a string of bells.
She finds shells and some old beads.

She even makes
a little Mary Mary!

One day, Lulu sees tiny green shoots!

She pulls up weeds
so the shoots can grow.

As the weather gets warmer,
Lulu's flowers open up to the sun.

Daddy helps Lulu
hang her shiny bells.

She puts her shells and beads in a row
and finds a special spot for Mary Mary.
It's just perfect!

Orla, Ben and Tayo are coming
to see Lulu's garden.
Lulu and Mummy make cupcakes.

Lulu puts on her favourite flower top
and Mummy helps do her hair.

Lulu's friends love everything about her garden.

They share the crunchy peas
and sweet strawberries
that Mummy grew.

Then Lulu decides to make up a new story about Mary Mary.

What will Lulu think of next!

Lulu, Lulu, extraordinary,
How does your garden grow?
With flower seeds,
And shells and beads,
And happy friends all in a row.

alanna books
...because everyone loves a good story

Everybody loves Lulu - critics, journalists, teachers, librarians, booksellers, parents and especially young children. They especially respond to how she and her family love books and stories and the way they inspire Lulu's play and imagination - whatever she does in life, Lulu consults a book!

Lulu loves Tuesdays. That's when she and her mummy go to the library. Lulu goes to story time and singing time. Then she chooses books for mummy to read at bedtime.

"A joyful exploration of books, libraries and sharing stories - this should be available in every library and children's centre." - Annie Everall

"I love this book and I want all library staff to have one." - Kath Navratil, EY Librarian

Paperback & Free multi-language CD - Listen to the story told in over 20 languages - perfect for inclusive storytimes   ISBN 978-0-9551998-20   £7.99 For ages 3 and up
Hardcover & CD ISBN 978-1-907825-071   £12.99 For ages 3 and up • Board book with shorter, simpler text ISBN 978-0-9551998-75   £4.99 For 4 months and up

Lulu loves stories - each night she reads a different one, and next day she is a fairy, a pilot, a farmer, a mummy, a tiger and a monster!

"An excellent jumping off point for so many reading activities. Having read the story, children will enjoy finding books about princesses, pilots, farmers, friendship, builders and especially 'wild and wicked monsters' for themselves." - Teaching with Picture Books

Paperback & Free multi-language CD - Listen to the story told in over 20 languages - perfect for inclusive storytimes   ISBN 978-1-907825-019   £8.99 For ages 3 and up
Hardcover ISBN 978-0-9551998-51   £9.99 For ages 3 and up • Board book with shorter, simpler text ISBN 978-1-907825-002   £4.99 For 4 months and up

From bath time to nap time, Lulu knows just the right story to read to new baby Zeki.

"This is a book I would recommend to all parents. A big 5 stars!" - Goodreads

"Excellent. This will be at the top of my list for recommending from the 'new baby' genre. Great addition to the series and stands alone well, too." - Goodreads

Paperback ISBN 978-1-907825-057   £6.99 For ages 3 and up • Hardcover ISBN 978-1-907825-040   £11.99 For ages 3 and up

And look out for Lulu's baby brother, Zeki - off on his own adventures!

"This brilliant and empowering book... perfectly reflects a baby's life, is warmly drawn, diverse, inclusive and just lovely. A must have for every nursery and playgroup." - Zoe Toft, Playing by the Book

"Books of the Year 2014! A copy should be given to all new parents." - Books for Keeps

ISBN 978-1-907825-101
24 toddler-friendly and robust card pages £7.99 For ages 1 and up

ISBN 978-1-907825-132
24 toddler-friendly and robust card pages £7.99 For ages 1 and up

www.alannabooks.com